Oddies®

This book
belongs to:

Matthew

....

Oddies Limited, Maritime House, Grafton Square, London, SW4 0JW
www.oddieworld.com

A CIP catalogue record for this book is available from the British Library.

First Published in Great Britain in 2004 by Oddies Limited.

ISBN 1-904745-14-8

Printed in Great Britain

Footy
Oddie

Grant Slatter

The footballer put his favourite pair of socks into the washing machine. He added some washing powder and shut the door.

"Chug-chug, whirr, chug-chug, whirr," went the washing machine. Then it did something strange.

It spun extra fast and all the bubbles bounced around wildly. The machine ballooned. Then there was a supersonic WHOOSH as one of the socks disappeared.

The sock was called Footy Oddie and he was zooming through space towards Oddieworld. "I hope it's sunny there - then we can have a game of football," he said.

Footy Oddie floated down into Oddieworld and popped out of his bubble. It was raining. "Please can you help me stop this rain?" said a soft voice behind him.

It was Sock Fairy. "The rain clouds are coming from Bad Oddie Island over there," she said. Footy Oddie looked round but when he turned back Sock Fairy had disappeared.

A shiny new football had appeared in her place. "What a gift," said Footy Oddie. "If I can stop this rain we *can* have a game of football."

Footy Oddie was just wondering how he could get to Bad Oddie Island when a boat appeared. "Hi Sailor Oddie," he shouted. "Fancy a trip to Bad Oddie Island?"

"Not really," said Sailor Oddie. "The whales are very playful today and there are pirates about. Mind you, I am a footy fan, so I'll take you!"

They set off in the boat and were sailing along when there was a big splash next to the boat.

"Was that a whale?" said Footy. "No!" said Sailor Oddie. "It was a cannon ball from that pirate ship!"

The pirates sailed nearer and fired another shot.

"Stop firing!" shouted Footy Oddie. "We're trying to get to Bad Oddie Island to stop this rain."

"In that case I'll take you there myself, sunshine!" said Captain Pirate Oddie. "This rain is making our gunpowder soggy."

Then he jumped down into Sailor Oddie's boat.

Soon they arrived at Bad Oddie Island. "Now listen good," growled Captain Pirate Oddie. "Witchy is on top of that hill boiling a rain potion."

"You won't be able to reach her though - it's too slippery!" he added, then roared with laughter. "It's one-nil to the Bad Oddies!"

The same thing happened each time he tried. Then he heard a voice behind him. "Move out of the way, please."

It was Wizzo. "This is a job for a spell expert," he said.
"Maybe it *is* time for a substitution," said Footy Oddie.

Wizzo whispered the magic words...

Watchmus Rain Blot,
knock down that pot!

There was a big bang
and a puff of smoke.

Wizzo now had his own mini rain cloud, which followed him as he hurried off. He didn't notice that his new pocket watch had vanished.

"If only I could knock that pot over," said Footy Oddie. Then he had a brilliant idea – a hot shot might do it!

He popped his football up...

...headed it down...

...and kicked it hard.

It scorched upward and hit Witchy's pot. There was a thunderous bang as the pot exploded.

Witchy slid down the hill.
"You won't get me with a slide-tackle," said Footy Oddie.

The rain stopped at last.
"Thanks Footy Oddie," said a familiar voice.

"I'd like to stay," said Footy Oddie. "I'm going to find those pirates and see if they want a game of football – there's a score to settle!"

The two sides met on Good Oddie Island.

Police Oddie started the match by blowing his whistle.
It didn't make a sound but a dog barked and
everyone laughed.

Pirates v Footy's Friends

Footy Oddie scored two goals, including the winner!

Back home, the footballer searched until midnight for his missing sock.

As he got into bed he asked himself...

"Where do those odd socks go?"

Have you got the complete collection?

Footy Oddie is the fourth book in the Oddies series. Read the stories of all the other Oddies and their adventures in Oddieworld.

The signposts on Good Oddie Island are all muddled up so Sock Fairy sends for **Police Oddie** - but he soon needs to call for help himself!

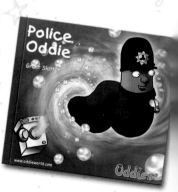

The secret is out, odd socks go to Oddieworld! Find out how Oddieworld was formed and how **Wizzo**, **Witchy** and **Sock Fairy** became stuck there.

Good Oddie River has dried up so Sock Fairy sends for **Rugby Oddie** - but only good teamwork can solve this problem.

Witchy wants the Oddie Crown Jewels and calls **Robber Oddie** to help her get them - but he soon learns that crime doesn't pay.

Litterbug has a tummy ache and nobody knows why, so Sock Fairy sends for **Nurse Oddie** - but can she make this patient better in a tick?

Every Oddie has a story to tell!

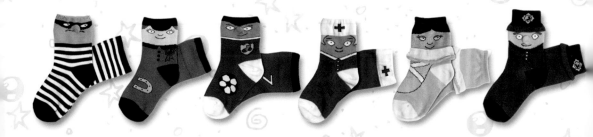

There are lots of
games to play plus
one secret game!

Find it and complete it
and we'll send you a
FREE Oddies poster!

Be quick and you can
win one of the last,
original artwork,
Oddies posters
like this one.

www.**oddieworld**.com

Please Note: Use of this website may permanently IMPROVE your
child's hand/eye co-ordination and intelligence!

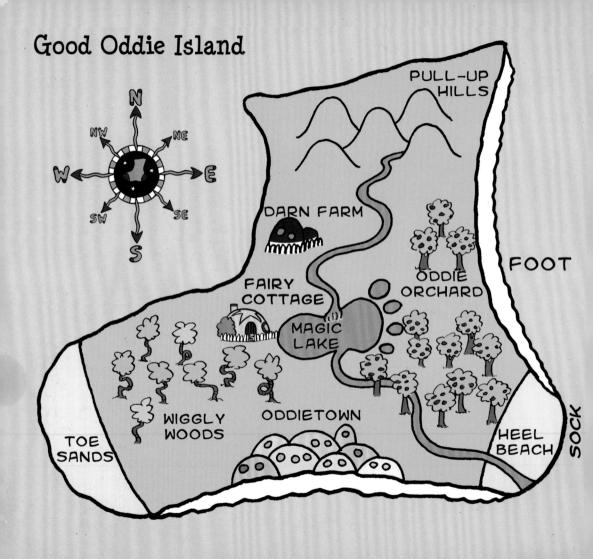